FRANKENSTEIN

This is a work of fiction. All of the characters, events, and organizations portrayed in this work are either products of the authors' imagination or used fictitiously.

Frankenstein

Adapted from the novel by Mary Wollstonecraft Shelley

ISBN-13: 978-1944540968

Published by Sordelet Ink
WWW.SORDELETINK.COM

FRANKENSTEIN

A PLAY BY
ROBERT KAUZLARIC

ADAPTED FROM THE NOVEL BY
Mary Wollstonecraft Shelley

Frankenstein received its world premiere at Lifeline Theatre in Chicago, IL, on September 17, 2018. It was directed by Paul S. Holmquist; the production stage manager was Becky Bishop; original music and sound design were by Barry Bennett; properties design was by Emily Hartig; costume design was by Izumi Inaba; the assistant stage manager was Anna Jones; lighting design was by Jordan Kardasz; fight direction was by Greg Poljacik; the production dramaturg was Maren Robinson; scenic design was by Joe Schermoly; and puppet design was by Cynthia Von Orthal. The cast was as follows:

Victoria—Ann Sonneville
Alphonse—Chris Hainsworth
Caroline—Risha Tenae
Erich—Ty Carter
Helena—Rasika Ranganathan
Justine—Emily Ayre
William—Trent Davis

Understudies—Sarah Kmiecik, Julie Partyka, Xander Senechal & Lauren Grace Thompson

The following credit must appear in all programs/playbills handed to audience members at performances of *Frankenstein*:

This adaptation of *Frankenstein* was originally produced by Lifeline Theatre (Chicago, IL) in 2018.

Cast of Characters

Victoria

Alphonse (her father)

Caroline (her mother)

Erich (her lover)

Helena (her friend)

Justine (her sister)

William (her brother)

The Creature (a puppet operated by the ensemble)

The Priest is performed by the actor playing Alphonse. Other roles, as needed, are played by the ensemble: professors, students, court officials, townsfolk, wedding guests, etc.

Setting

The action of the play takes place in a dreamlike middle ground between reality and Victoria's internal experience. Certain events should be understood to literally happen (Alphonse's death, for example) but many can be an open question in the audience's mind (such as later character deaths).

The set should represent a grim retreat from reality: a crumbling depository of shattered memories and broken relics of home, family, and father. In the original production, the space suggested an old attic, filled with detritus, floating in an inky void, but other visuals could be equally evocative of Victoria's mental state.

At the heart of the space there is an open grave. Whether it is always visible or revealed as needed, its placement should represent a focal point, a void, a constant reminder.

The play takes place in an unrelenting present tense. The time period of costuming and properties should feel hard to pin down. No dialects should be used by the actors. The story should feel like it's either happening now or always happening, and that it's happening here.

Adaptor's Note

After the death of his wife, C.S. Lewis wrote in his diary, "No one ever told me that grief felt so like fear."

When my father died unexpectedly, I grew obsessed with the contemplation of grief. And the grieving process. It haunts me. I think about it every day, and I long suspected that I had a project specifically about grief in me, just waiting to surface.

Then, several years ago, I re-read *Frankenstein* and I knew at once it would be the vehicle for what I wanted to explore. And the more I learned about Mary Shelley and the unspeakable losses she suffered while writing and revising her novel (multiple children, her sister, her husband), the more I saw in the story a metaphor for a grief experience: a death leads to the birth of a powerful force that the protagonist can't control. They run from it, lash out at it, try to bargain with it or pretend it doesn't exist. But they never come to accept it.

And so it destroys them.

When I began to imagine an adaptation, I envisioned my Creature as a living personification of Grief and how it haunts our lives. How it assaults us. How it demands more from us than we can give. How it can overwhelm us with feelings of guilt or persecution, and drives us from the ones we love. I imagined it growing in strength and power as it consumed more and more of its creator's psyche. I imagined a dreamlike experience. An unsettling immersion. An emotional journey rather than a literal one.

An allegory.

We had a lot of conversations about grief during the process of creating this show. It was fascinating to hear the designers and actors talk about their experiences and traditions and rituals. It made me realize how little we actually talk – meaningfully and personally – about death and grief, despite how much of it we're surrounded by. My hope is that this piece will engender some conversations about grief: what it is, what it feels like, what it does to us. How it can truly mess us up. And how we find our way through it.

(As the audience enters the theatre, they discover VICTORIA onstage. She wears black clothing of an indeterminate period, possibly from 1800, possibly from yesterday. She sits with a well-worn journal among collected relics of home, family, and father. Perhaps she writes. Perhaps she draws. Perhaps she catalogues the detritus that surrounds her.)

(As the play begins, a single light rises on VICTORIA, drawing her out of her activity. She talks directly to the audience.)

VICTORIA
Nothing is so painful to the human mind as a great and sudden change.

(The sound of birds is heard. VICTORIA looks to the heavens.)

VICTORIA
The sun may shine. Birds may sing. But nothing appears as it had before.

(CAROLINE becomes visible in silhouette.)

CAROLINE
(Gentle) Victoria.

(A bell tolls in the distance.)

VICTORIA
How strangely our souls are constructed. By such slight ligaments are we bound to prosperity... or ruin.

CAROLINE
(Insistent) Victoria.

(The bell tolls again, loud and close.)

VICTORIA
This is where everything begins. With an ending.

CAROLINE
What words can I use? How can I tell you? It is impossible. Victoria, your father is dead. He passed calmly, and his eyes expressed the deepest affection, even to the last.

(Music begins, softly at first. It continues throughout the play, changing and evolving with each new scene, a defining element of the emotional life of the piece.)

(VICTORIA embraces CAROLINE. As they embrace, they collapse to the floor.)

(ERICH, HELENA, JUSTINE, and WILLIAM appear and come together in support of VICTORIA and each other. VICTORIA is barely aware of them. As lights evolve, it becomes clear that their clothing is timeless in a manner similar to VICTORIA's. CAROLINE wears a small portrait brooch with a gold frame and JUSTINE wears a cross on a chain about her neck.)

ERICH
Your father was respected by all who knew him.

JUSTINE
He was so gentle, so wise.

HELENA
He had so much more to teach us.

WILLIAM
He was so strong.

CAROLINE
He loved so fiercely.

JUSTINE
Victoria?

ERICH
Victoria, where are you?

HELENA
What are you feeling?

VICTORIA
(Out) I feel nothing.

CAROLINE
Victoria, where are you?

VICTORIA
(Out) They speak words.

JUSTINE
We will survive this.

VICTORIA
(Out) But their words are meaningless. They talk of the future.

ERICH
The time will come when your father—

VICTORIA
They talk of the past.

HELENA
Do you remember when your father—

VICTORIA
They mean well; they do. They are possessed by the very spirit of compassion.

(VICTORIA removes herself from the family picture.)

VICTORIA
But ever since childhood, my temper has been singular, my passions vehement. For some living beneath the shadow of death, there is comfort to be found everywhere. *(She looks up at the family, now a shadowy collection of faceless figures.)* For others, nowhere.

(Lightning strikes. It begins to rain. The family gathers around an open grave, holding each other for comfort as they huddle beneath umbrellas and take turns reading from a bible. A PRIEST joins them, though he faces upstage and is only barely seen. VICTORIA remains apart.)

PRIEST
We are gathered to honor the memory of a beloved father.

VICTORIA
The rites and rituals proceed as they always do.

ERICH
(Reading) The just man, though he die early, shall be at rest.

VICTORIA
Old words. Empty ideas. I try to be present.

ERICH
(Reading) For the souls of the just are in the hand of God …

VICTORIA
To be with them.

ERICH
(Reading) …and no torment shall touch them.

VICTORIA
But here at the crossroads of faith and death… I am with him.

(The PRIEST turns and he is now ALPHONSE, wearing a dark suit of an indeterminate period. The family continues the service, unaware, as VICTORIA moves through space with him, creating images expressing their history and love for one another. As they move, the darkness above the stage fills with stars.)

VICTORIA
We are unfashioned creatures, only half made up, without the one who is wiser, stronger, better than ourselves… to help us be wiser, stronger, and better than we are.

CAROLINE
(Reading) My soul is deprived of peace.

VICTORIA
He saw me. As I was. As I dreamed I could be.

CAROLINE
(Reading) I have forgotten what happiness is.

VICTORIA
When I glowed with the enthusiasm of success, he shared in my joy.

CAROLINE
(Reading) I tell myself the future is lost.

VICTORIA
When I was assailed by dejection, he sustained me.

CAROLINE
(Reading) And this thought is wormwood and gall...

VICTORIA
The seasons turned.

CAROLINE
(Reading) ...as I remember it over and over...

HELENA
And over and over...

VICTORIA
Our lives evolved.

JUSTINE
Over and over...

WILLIAM
Over and over...

VICTORIA
And through it all, my father was there.

(All falls still. VICTORIA regards ALPHONSE.)

VICTORIA
The stars do not more certainly shine in the heavens than did my belief that his love was eternal.

(Distant thunder rumbles. The family ushers ALPHONSE into the grave.)

VICTORIA
But love is terrible. Love is cruel. Love can leave us. In

the roar of violence, in the silence of a whisper.

JUSTINE
(Reading) And so the mighty ruler prepared a purifying sacrifice. And why did he do this?

CAROLINE, ERICH, HELENA & WILLIAM
Resurrection.

(This word strikes a chord in VICTORIA. She engages with the ceremony for the first time.)

VICTORIA
Resurrection?

JUSTINE
(Reading) For he knew the Lord would work a miracle. The fallen would rise again. And all would see him.

CAROLINE, ERICH, HELENA & WILLIAM
With their own eyes.

JUSTINE
(Reading) Those who sleep in the earth shall awake. Some shall be an everlasting horror. But others shall shine brightly, like the splendor of the firmament...

CAROLINE, ERICH, HELENA, JUSTINE & WILLIAM
And be like stars. Forever.

(The family departs. VICTORIA is alone with the grave as the stars shine overhead.)

VICTORIA
When our dearest ties are rent with such finality, there is a void that presents itself to the soul. It is impossible for the mind to persuade itself that he whose existence was inextricably entwined with our own can have departed forever...

(VICTORIA sees something of ALPHONSE somewhere else on the set, perhaps his face reflected in a shard of broken mirror, perhaps a familiar shadow cast upon a wall.)

ALPHONSE
(A whisper) Victoria...

VICTORIA
...that the brightness of his eye has been extinguished... that the sound of his voice has been hushed...

(She sees him in a new location.)

ALPHONSE
Victoria...

VICTORIA
...and so we see him, and we hear him...

(She sees him in a new location.)

ALPHONSE
Victoria...

VICTORIA
...wherever we go.

(VICTORIA forcibly blocks out the world, the grave, and the visions.)

VICTORIA
But the time comes when grief is rather an indulgence than a necessity. I have duties to perform. I will... I will... I will return to school.

(VICTORIA grabs her journal and tries to depart, but the family appears and wherever she turns, they block her path.)

CAROLINE, ERICH, HELENA, JUSTINE & WILLIAM
Don't go.

VICTORIA
I can't stay here.

ERICH
Victoria.

VICTORIA
I must continue my education.

CAROLINE
Victoria, I need you.

JUSTINE
Your brother needs you.

HELENA
The family needs you.

VICTORIA
I must continue—

CAROLINE
Victoria. The property.

JUSTINE
The will.

ERICH
The estate.

CAROLINE
The money.

WILLIAM
The lawyers.

HELENA
The letters.

JUSTINE
The arrangements.

CAROLINE
The deeds.

ERICH
The details.

HELENA
The visits.

WILLIAM
The family.

VICTORIA
I can't.

CAROLINE, ERICH, HELENA, JUSTINE & WILLIAM
Stay!

VICTORIA
I won't!

(VICTORIA cries out and banishes her family. Only CAROLINE remains. VICTORIA collapses into her arms.)

CAROLINE
Survive this. Do what you have to. Tell yourself what you need to. But survive this. I can't lose both of you.

VICTORIA
I'll try, mom.

CAROLINE
Promise me.

(VICTORIA nods. CAROLINE departs.)

VICTORIA
I retreat.

(The scene shifts. VICTORIA stands motionless at the center of a shadowy swirl of forms and figures living their lives around her, not touching her, not reaching her. Occasionally, glimpses and hints of ALPHONSE can be seen amongst the shapes that pass by her.)

VICTORIA
I return to school. Where nothing has changed, yet I recognize nothing. And no one. The world has moved on. Or I have. I cannot tell. My life has become a foreign country. The clothing is strange. I don't speak the language.

ALPHONSE
Victoria...

VICTORIA
So I retreat.

(The scene shifts, growing darker, tunneling in further.)

VICTORIA
The days pass. I shun my fellow students as if guilty of a crime. I retreat further and further. Deeper and deeper inside.

(Another shift, and VICTORIA is alone under a single light.)

VICTORIA
School falls away. The world falls away. But my loved ones... they write to me. It starts with my mother.

(CAROLINE appears. VICTORIA partially listens to her, but most of her attention is spent leafing through the pages of her journal.)

CAROLINE
I've spent the past weeks revisiting the letters we

received after the funeral. All your father's friends, his clients, people I never even met. They talk of his kindness. His compassion. All true. So true. But we mustn't forget the times he failed us. The times he failed himself. He was only a man. There were flaws. There were shadows. But it's the details—the sum of those details—that make up the truth of a life. And we must honor his truth, his whole truth, as we look for the strength to move forward.

VICTORIA
Move forward?

CAROLINE
Remember your promise to me. And come home soon.

VICTORIA
The more she says, the clearer it becomes. She views his death as a reality. A truth to define her future. A truth I must accept. Justine tries next.

(JUSTINE appears. Again, VICTORIA splits her attention between JUSTINE and the journal.)

JUSTINE
Sweet sister, I've been thinking of you and reflecting on the story of Naomi... *(Reading from a Bible)* "The Lord has brought misfortune upon me." Yes. He has. But that's not how the story ends. I can't stop thinking about those ten little words: "She found herself working in a field belonging to Boaz." And the future they promise. The hope. "Naomi laid the child in her lap and cared for him." We are Naomi. And we are the child. And I know one day soon God will wipe every tear from our eyes. And we'll move forward. Together.

VICTORIA
Move forward...

JUSTINE
I pray for you, Victoria.

VICTORIA
Don't pray for me.

JUSTINE
That you'll find peace.

VICTORIA
They want to release him. To let him go. They are weak. I must be strong. Stronger than them. Stronger than these feelings. Stronger than death itself. Since God wouldn't save him with a miracle, I must create a miracle of my own. I go to work.

(Referencing notes from her journal, VICTORIA begins to travel the space, pulling tokens, relics, and shards of memory from the rubble, piling them by the grave. Music builds as her passion and intensity grow.)

VICTORIA
I gather souvenirs and tokens. Relics. Mementos. Evidence of a life.

(HELENA appears. VICTORIA continues to work, barely aware of her presence.)

HELENA
Victoria, I know exactly what you need: let's run away!

VICTORIA
Like we did when we were kids?

HELENA
Only this time I won't make us dress like wandering knights. And we'll get further than the end of the stream. This time, we'll cross the continent! Climb over mountains. Dance in the ocean. We'll light fires, meet strang-

ers, eat and drink and laugh and cry. We'll put some distance between ourselves and the old memories. By making new ones. Today is a gift, a precious one. Take a semester off and join me!

VICTORIA
As I work, the various keys which form the mechanism of my soul are touched, chord after chord is sounded, and my heart is filled with a symphony comprised of one thought, one purpose. Resurrection.

(VICTORIA begins to assemble the collected relics, attaching them, combining them, forming the rough shape of a man lying upon the ground. The stars grow brighter in the heavens.)

VICTORIA
By the light of the stars, I work. From the ashes, I build. A frantic impulse urges me on and I am powerless to resist. It carries me forward with the force of a hurricane, crushing everything in its path.

(WILLIAM and ERICH appear.)

WILLIAM
Mother wanted me to write. She thinks it will help you stop feeling so sad about father. I don't remember father. Not really. But I remember a feeling. Erich says...

ERICH
That's love.

WILLIAM
He says it feels different for everyone... and with everyone...

ERICH
But you'll recognize that feeling, William, because it feels like... tomorrow's worth living for.

WILLIAM
I try to think about father, but I don't have a picture in my head anymore. So mother gave me one.

(CAROLINE gives WILLIAM the miniature portrait.)

VICTORIA
She gave away his portrait...

WILLIAM
I like it. He looks nice. Like a dad. We walk through the woods a lot lately, me and mother and Justine. Justine says...

JUSTINE
You should be mindful of God on our walks, for here, in the quiet, growing places of the world you can feel Him most dearly.

WILLIAM
I tell her I do. But mostly I'm mindful of the rabbits. Have you seen how they leap? But sometimes when we pass a place...

CAROLINE
This is where he took you fishing. This is where you rode the old sled.

WILLIAM
I get a feeling. It's a good feeling. It feels like rabbits, jumping in the grass. So I run. Through the grass. And they fuss at me.

CAROLINE & JUSTINE
William!

WILLIAM
But I'm the rabbit. And I'll never, ever be caught!

(VICTORIA finishes her creation. It is both beautiful

and grotesque.)

VICTORIA
They have nothing to offer me. They are content to settle. To move on. They are weak. I must be strong. I will do what none of them dare.

(VICTORIA takes up a glass container containing an unlit candle.)

VICTORIA
I will break the boundaries between here and the hereafter and pour a torrent of light into this sad and bitter world.

ERICH
My dearest, do you remember the estate near the lakeshore where we used to walk before you left for university? I mentioned how every great house has a name, and I called it Hornbeam for the trees that enclose it.

VICTORIA
For which I teased you mercilessly.

ERICH
You wanted to name it Violet House.

VICTORIA
For the hue the western wall takes at dusk.

ERICH
The house is for sale. I walk past it now, sometimes alone, sometimes with William. And as I watch him run through the tall grass...

WILLIAM
I'm the rabbit!

ERICH
I think of the vow we made, to raise our own children in those fields.

WILLIAM
You'll never catch me!

ERICH
And I look forward with a full heart to a future built by your side.

VICTORIA
Enough!

(She gestures and all falls still.)

VICTORIA
It's time. Now something beautiful will come to life, something only I could make.

(ALPHONSE rises from the grave. The stars blaze to life in the heavens.)

VICTORIA
For these memories are mine and mine alone. And they are precious and boundless and... miraculous. Something beautiful will come to life and it will bless me as its source. It will be mine. It will be eternal. It will be—

(Lights shift and the family reaches out to VICTORIA.)

CAROLINE, ERICH, HELENA, JUSTINE & WILLIAM
Victoria, stop!

VICTORIA
It seems to me as if guardian angels appear to avert the coming storm.

(A bell sounds. VICTORIA looks to the heavens.)

VICTORIA
How strangely our souls are constructed. By such slight ligaments are we bound to prosperity... or ruin.

CAROLINE, ERICH, HELENA, JUSTINE & WILLIAM
There is another way.

VICTORIA
It is a strong effort by the spirits of good. But ultimately ineffectual.

(She gestures and the family fades into the shadows. She clutches her container close.)

VICTORIA
I capture my memories. Memories from childhood, from my youth, from adolescence. Moments large and small. A look. A laugh. A lesson. These will empower me, fuel my great design. I remember.

(She closes her eyes and draws a breath. A star dims in the night sky. When she exhales, her candle flickers faintly to life.)

VICTORIA
I remember.

(She breathes in and out, extinguishing more stars and increasing the intensity of her candle.)

VICTORIA
I remember.

(During the following, the rest of the stars dim until the candle blazes like a sun.)

VICTORIA
I recount every embrace, every tear, every joy, which formed the foundation of a love so fundamental to... me... to myself... to my sense of place in this world. And as I capture these memories, my destiny arises, like a mountain river from an unseen spring, to sweep away these sensations, these feelings, this future I cannot bear.

(VICTORIA places the candle into the heart of her creation. ALPHONSE becomes operator for the CREATURE. The puppet will ultimately be articulated by six people, so at first its operation is ungainly. During the following, the family remains at the edges of the light, shadowy figures witnessing the scene. VICTORIA rises to her feet, raises her arms, and an earth-shaking blast of lightning strikes the CREATURE. It opens its eyes and comes to life. It rises painfully to its feet, towering over VICTORIA, and voices a wordless expression of agony. This is a long, unsettling moment.)

VICTORIA
Father...?

(VICTORIA reaches for the CREATURE. The CREATURE suddenly grabs her arm.)

CREATURE (ALPHONSE)
Your father is dead.

(Thunder and lightning. VICTORIA screams as the CREATURE pulls her into a desperate embrace. It howls in pain and confusion, expressing the one sentiment it knows with certainty at this moment, over and over.)

CREATURE (ALPHONSE)
Your father is dead. Your father is dead.

VICTORIA
Help! Help me!

(The embrace grows more fearsome and VICTORIA appears at risk of becoming absorbed inside of her creation. Finally, she extracts herself and scrambles away from the CREATURE.)

VICTORIA
What are you?

(Lurching and in pain, the CREATURE stalks Victoria. Its posture is broken and bent. Only some of its limbs function correctly.)

CREATURE (ALPHONSE)
Help me.

VICTORIA
That is not his face.

CREATURE (ALPHONSE)
This is the face you gave me.

VICTORIA
That is not his body.

CREATURE (ALPHONSE)
This is the form you gave me.

VICTORIA
It was supposed to be beautiful. This is a mockery! An insult to my father's memory!

(The CREATURE attempts to embrace VICTORIA again. After another struggle, she escapes.)

CREATURE (ALPHONSE)
Help me!

VICTORIA
I can't help you. I... I can't even look at you.

CREATURE (ALPHONSE)
Help me!

VICTORIA
No one can help you.

CREATURE (ALPHONSE)
Then I have nothing.

VICTORIA
I have nothing!

(VICTORIA wails in desperation, deeply affecting the CREATURE. The family moves in and gathers close to VICTORIA.)

CAROLINE, ERICH, HELENA, JUSTINE & WILLIAM
(Overlap, not unison) Victoria.

VICTORIA
What have I done? All that time, all that pain... For what? I have nothing. Nothing. Nothing but... this.

CAROLINE
You have a family.

JUSTINE
You are surrounded by love.

VICTORIA
My angels...

CREATURE (ALPHONSE)
Noooooo!

(The CREATURE pushes VICTORIA's family out of the light and deep into shadow.)

CAROLINE, ERICH, HELENA, JUSTINE & WILLIAM
(A cascading overlap, not unison) Victoria?

VICTORIA
I can't see them anymore. Where are they?

CAROLINE, ERICH, HELENA, JUSTINE & WILLIAM
(Overlapping, barely seen from the shadows) We're right here!

CREATURE (ALPHONSE)
No. Those are just shadows.

CAROLINE
My child.

VICTORIA
Mother…

CREATURE (ALPHONSE)
That is not your mother. Your mother doesn't care. Your mother has moved on. That is a shadow. Nothing more. They all are.

VICTORIA
It's my—

CREATURE (ALPHONSE)
It's not your mother. It's just an idea.

VICTORIA
No, she's my connection to the past!

(The CREATURE gestures and CAROLINE sinks to the floor.)

VICTORIA
But she's so faint now…

ERICH
My love.

VICTORIA
Erich?

CREATURE (ALPHONSE)
That's not Erich. It's not even real.

VICTORIA
No…

ERICH
My dearest.

VICTORIA
He's real. My parents took him in as a child. We grew up together. I remember!

CREATURE (ALPHONSE)
It's nothing. A figment.

VICTORIA
He is my hope for the future. He has to be real!

(The CREATURE gestures and ERICH sinks to the floor.)

HELENA
Victoria.

VICTORIA
Oh, Helena... my best friend.

CREATURE (ALPHONSE)
No. It's nothing.

VICTORIA
She's my joy, my happiness.

(The CREATURE gestures and HELENA sinks to the floor.)

JUSTINE & WILLIAM
Sister.

VICTORIA
Justine.

CREATURE (ALPHONSE)
She's not real!

VICTORIA
Yes, she is! My parents saved her from an abusive home.

CREATURE (ALPHONSE)
No.

VICTORIA
She taught me what I know about God.

CREATURE (ALPHONSE)
You know nothing.

VICTORIA
She's my faith. And William! My little brother...

(The CREATURE gestures and JUSTINE and WILLIAM sink to the floor.)

VICTORIA
My innocence.

CREATURE (ALPHONSE)
They! Are! Nothing!

(The CREATURE roars and the entire family vanishes.)

CREATURE (ALPHONSE)
It's just us now. Embrace me.

VICTORIA
No. Never.

CREATURE (ALPHONSE)
Then why did you make me?

VICTORIA
I... had to. I had to. I had to! There was nothing else I could do. I thought you would be—

CREATURE (ALPHONSE)
A torrent of light.

VICTORIA
Yes. Not a thing of darkness. I thought you would be—

CREATURE (ALPHONSE)
I am exactly as you made me.

VICTORIA
(Inspiration strikes, wild and feverish) If I made you, then I can unmake you!

CREATURE (ALPHONSE)
You cannot.

VICTORIA
Come here.

CREATURE (ALPHONSE)
No! You are mine! And I am yours!

VICTORIA
Mine to destroy! I will tear you limb from limb!

(VICTORIA assaults the CREATURE. It wails in misery.)

VICTORIA
Yes! Now you feel what I feel. Cry! Scream! May the sound of your lamentations never cease!

(The CREATURE lashes out, unintentionally knocking VICTORIA to the ground. Both are startled and hurt by its strength.)

CREATURE (ALPHONSE)
This is a sad and bitter world.

VICTORIA
Yes. This is a sad and bitter world.

CREATURE (ALPHONSE)
This... is a world of your own making.

(Thunder and lightning crack. The CREATURE flees into the night.)

VICTORIA
What have I done?

(VICTORIA climbs over the rubble to a filthy bed perched at an uncomfortable angle. She pulls back soiled sheets and slides into bed.)

VICTORIA
I seek forgetfulness. But it is in vain. Half awake, half asleep, I am tormented by hideous dreams. I see Erich, in the bloom of health, walking by the lakeshore. I rush to him... but as we kiss, his lips grow livid with the hue of death. His flesh withers. The light fades from his eyes. Flies and worms issue from his ears, his nose, his—

HELENA
(Offstage) Victoria?

(HELENA enters and joins VICTORIA at her bedside.)

VICTORIA
Helena? Why are you here?

HELENA
I came to take you away. Or to join your studies, if you're going to stay. Are you all right? *(She reaches out to touch VICTORIA.)*

VICTORIA
(Pulling away from her) No! You mustn't touch me! Who let you in? How... how did you get in the building?

HELENA
The front door was open—

VICTORIA
No, no, no, no! Is it real? Don't tell me it's real! It can't be real. What did you see?

HELENA
Where? When? Nothing.

VICTORIA
Nothing?

HELENA
Nothing.

VICTORIA
Are you real?

HELENA
What is it, Victoria? What's the matter?

VICTORIA
Don't ask me. Never ask me. Never speak of it!

(VICTORIA passes out. Months pass as HELENA nurses an ill and feverish VICTORIA. Finally, VICTORIA comes to herself again. She sits up and sees sunlight streaming through a window and HELENA sleeping beside her bed.)

VICTORIA
What... what day is it?

HELENA
(Stirring awake) A new one. A new beginning.

VICTORIA
Oh, Helena, how good you are to me. All this time, shut up in my sick room. How can I ever repay you?

(VICTORIA rises from her bed. She is weak and needs help from HELENA.)

HELENA
You will repay me by not overtaxing yourself.

VICTORIA
Of course.

HELENA
And your family would be very happy to hear from you. Especially Erich; he feels he can't leave your mother alone with William and Justine. She's still not ready. But it's killing him that he can't be at your side.

VICTORIA
Yes! I will write instantly.

HELENA
And when you are well enough to travel—

VICTORIA
Of course! Soon! Very soon! Helena...

HELENA
Yes?

VICTORIA
Nothing... happened while I was ill, did it?

HELENA
Happened?

VICTORIA
Forgive me. A dream I had. Lingering nightmares, nothing more.

(VICTORIA enters a manic period. She moves objects from place to place and rearranges things in a way that seems meaningful to her but results in no perceptible difference.)

VICTORIA
None of it happened. I can start again. The slate is clean. I can move forward. Just like they said I should. I reorder my life. I am in control. I am well. I am healthy.

HELENA
Victoria—

VICTORIA
Soon!

(Time passes. VICTORIA brings HELENA before a shadowy cabal of robed PROFESSORS.)

VICTORIA
I am in control. I am well. I introduce Helena to the proper professors. She's here, at university, after all, and now she can channel her passions for the old stories—the Knights of the Round Table, the Erinyes, Grendel and his mother—into something new. Something beautiful. She lost so much time caring for me. This will not stand!

(The PROFESSORS begin issuing forth a large number of books, handing them to VICTORIA. VICTORIA presses the first few into HELENA's hands.)

HELENA
Victoria—

VICTORIA
Soon!

(Time passes. As more and more books issue forth, VICTORIA stacks them into a structure, walling herself off.)

VICTORIA
I am well. I move forward. Leaving my former studies behind, I join Helena in obsessively consuming tales of bygone times. They speak to me from across the centuries. Their melancholy is soothing; their joy elevating. What's old becomes new… *(She is briefly struck by the resemblance of one of the PROFESSORS to her father.)* What's dead finds new life in my imagination. *(She shakes off the feeling.)* I am well. I am well. I am—

HELENA
Victoria—

VICTORIA
Soon!

(VICTORIA sits within her fortress of books, moving neither forward nor backward. She chooses to believe she is content. Finally, HELENA finds a way through to break VICTORIA free.)

VICTORIA
Time passes and I move forward. Rather, I am moved forward. Study secludes me from the intercourse of society, but Helena calls forth the better feelings of my heart. She teaches me to love the sun again, and the cheerful faces of students. We see in all things what we choose to see, and what I see is now sunlight and—

HELENA
Victoria, you must go home.

VICTORIA
Soon, my friend; soon!

(She crosses away. HELENA follows.)

VICTORIA
I fix my visit home, but the roads are impassable.

HELENA
(Taking hold of VICTORIA) You can put off your family no longer.

VICTORIA
I have put no one off! I've simply—

HELENA
Enough. It's been over a year now.

(Finally, VICTORIA stops.)

VICTORIA
A year? I've... I have not been ready.

HELENA
(Taking VICTORIA's hand) You can do this.

VICTORIA
I don't deserve you, Helena.

HELENA
You deserve all that's good.

VICTORIA
I'm almost ready. I just need a little more time.

(HELENA embraces her and exits.)

VICTORIA
To find the necessary strength, my soul drives me to a change of place. So I bend myself toward the mountains, seeking in their magnificence to put to rest, at last, the shadow hanging over my soul.

(VICTORIA climbs a section of the detritus resembling a mountain range. She grows stronger and more confident as she goes, but occasionally senses a presence stalking behind her.)

VICTORIA
The weather is glorious. The roar of the river rushes in time with the pounding of my heart. I ascend higher. The peaks surround me, mighty and sublime. The winds whisper in soothing accents. I stand at the source of the river, surrounded by scattered, shattered pines, and the solemn silence of imperial nature subdues my soul.

(VICTORIA moves aside pieces of the rubble heap to reveal a tidy, humble, one-room cottage—an oasis of

domesticity amidst the blasted landscape. Meanwhile, the CREATURE appears, entering by the same path VICTORIA followed. It is slightly larger now than it was before and moves more upright. Spying the cottage, it approaches stealthily. Finding a small chink in one of the walls, it presses its eye against it and watches VICTORIA in secret.)

VICTORIA
I take up in a remote cabin and strip myself of my cares, my daily concerns, my passions, and my desires. I seek solace in a simpler life. With simpler rules.

(VICTORIA lights a fire. At the edges of the glow, CAROLINE, ERICH, HELENA, JUSTINE, and WILLIAM appear, more menacing figures now than representations of specific people.)

VICTORIA
My spirits of good now manifest as angels of destruction. But they can possess only the strength I choose to give them.

(JUSTINE sets a bottle of liquor in front of VICTORIA.)

VICTORIA
All right.

(VICTORIA sits down with the bottle and drinks.)

VICTORIA
Take stock. What do I have... that is not despair?

CAROLINE, ERICH, HELENA, JUSTINE & WILLIAM
(A dark whisper) Nothing.

VICTORIA
I have my memories of the past.

CAROLINE
(A dark whisper) No.

VICTORIA
I have my hopes for the future.

ERICH
(A dark whisper) No.

VICTORIA
Yes. I have the joy I can find in the present.

HELENA
(A dark whisper) No.

VICTORIA
I have my faith.

JUSTINE
(A dark whisper) No.

VICTORIA
And I have—somewhere—I have my innocence. Some piece of it remains.

WILLIAM
You have nothing.

ERICH
Nothing but the stories you tell yourself.

(Night falls on the mountain. The figures move in closer as VICTORIA closes her eyes and tries to will them away.)

JUSTINE
Your dreams will poison your sleep.

CAROLINE
Your thoughts will pollute your days.

WILLIAM
Laugh or cry...

ERICH
Embrace your woes...

HELENA
Or cast your cares away...

JUSTINE
It's all the same.

CAROLINE
Yesterday is dead.

HELENA
Today is dying.

ERICH
Tomorrow will perish.

WILLIAM
There is nothing. But change.

(The fire dies out. VICTORIA drifts off to sleep and the figures disappear.)

(The CREATURE crosses to the door of the cottage and enters. VICTORIA stirs in her chair. Despite the faint moonlight, she can't see through the shadows in the doorway.)

VICTORIA
Who's there?

CREATURE (Alphonse)
Pardon my intrusion. And the lateness of the hour. But I am desperate. I am a traveler in want of a little rest. The night is cold and I'm all alone; you would greatly oblige me if you'd allow me to remain a few minutes.

VICTORIA
Of course. Let me see if I can find some food for you—

CREATURE (ALPHONSE)
Don't trouble yourself; it's only warmth and rest that I need.

VICTORIA
Where do you travel?

CREATURE (ALPHONSE)
I'm going to claim the protection of a friend. But I'm full of fears, for if I fail with them, I am an outcast in this world forever.

VICTORIA
To be friendless is indeed to be unfortunate, but if your friend is kind, do not despair.

CREATURE (ALPHONSE)
She was. Once. But where she ought to see a friend in me, she beholds only an enemy.

VICTORIA
Can you not undeceive her?

CREATURE (ALPHONSE)
I am about to undertake that task; and that is why I feel such fear. I desperately love this friend. I need her. And she needs me. We are one.

VICTORIA
Where does she reside?

CREATURE (ALPHONSE)
(It hesitates before speaking.) Near this spot.

VICTORIA
What is her name?

(The CREATURE struggles for a moment, then begins

to sob.)

VICTORIA
(Comforting) No, no; all will be well. Come, I'll find you some food.

(VICTORIA stands. The CREATURE steps in and becomes visible in the shaft of moonlight.)

VICTORIA
How did you find me!?

CREATURE (ALPHONSE)
You call to me. Awake, asleep, with every action, every breath.

(VICTORIA takes up a weapon—a poker from the fireplace or something similar.)

VICTORIA
Get out! You wretch! You monster!

CREATURE (ALPHONSE)
Why have you forsaken me? You are my maker; I ought to be your Adam, but rather I am the fallen angel. Everywhere I see bliss, from which I alone am excluded. Isolation and misery will turn me into a fiend. See me, hear me—help me!—and I can be virtuous.

VICTORIA
You have no right to bliss. You have no right to exist!

CREATURE (ALPHONSE)
The most terrible of villains are allowed to speak in their own defense before they are condemned. I ask you merely to hear me.

VICTORIA
(She battles with this decision, but eventually concedes.) Very well. Speak.

CREATURE (ALPHONSE)
You made me. And then you rejected me. So I fled. I fled from the light and sank into shadow. My solitude was a misery, the sufferings I endured intense. Your soul cried out to mine, but I could not have you. I began to fade into oblivion. But then I saw you. You! Here in the great emptiness! And so I followed you. And I watched you. And I listened. But I could not understand. You are made in God's image. You have a home. Food. Fire. You have a family. Then why are you unhappy? And if someone like you could be so... lost... how could a creature like myself hope for anything but eternal misery?

VICTORIA
(Unable to fully process what she's hearing) What are you?

CREATURE (ALPHONSE)
I am what you made me.

VICTORIA
I didn't know what I was making.

CREATURE (ALPHONSE)
You knew.

(Beat)

VICTORIA
I didn't—

CREATURE (ALPHONSE)
You. Knew.

VICTORIA
What do you want?

CREATURE (ALPHONSE)
Communion. Come, join me, and together we will stare into the terrible abyss of what it means to be human.

VICTORIA
You are not human.

CREATURE (ALPHONSE)
What it means to exist.

VICTORIA
What do you want from me?

CREATURE (ALPHONSE)
Take me into your life. Accept me as your creation.

VICTORIA
Never!

CREATURE (ALPHONSE)
Refuse me, and I shall destroy all that you love.

VICTORIA
I do refuse you. And no torture shall ever extort a consent from me.

CREATURE (ALPHONSE)
Then what will you do?

VICTORIA
I will go.

CREATURE (ALPHONSE)
Where will you go?

VICTORIA
School. Back to school.

CREATURE (ALPHONSE)
There is no school.

VICTORIA
Of course there is!

CREATURE (ALPHONSE)
There is no school. There are only the stories you tell

yourself.

VICTORIA
I am studying—

CREATURE (ALPHONSE)
Worlds within worlds.

VICTORIA
You don't know what you're—

CREATURE (ALPHONSE)
Lies within lies.

VICTORIA
I know what's real.

CREATURE (ALPHONSE)
You know only shadows.

VICTORIA
I know what's real!

CREATURE (ALPHONSE)
Am I real?

VICTORIA
No. Yes. No. I don't know…

CREATURE (ALPHONSE)
My need is real. And you will give me what I want. Whether you wish it or no. Because we're alone in here now, you and I. And soon, you will accept me. When there's nowhere else for you to turn.

(VICTORIA flees. She returns to school and immerses herself in the chaotic dance of society. HELENA tries to interpose herself before VICTORIA, but cannot secure her attention.)

VICTORIA
I'll go back to school, to the noise and the light, to the roiling chaos of the myriad crowds. *(Joining the dance.)* How foolish it was to seek peace in solitude! School will be my haven. The creature will not follow me here. It fears the light. A month passes. And then two. My greatest defense—my only defense!—lies in the safety of numbers. My one hope for—

(The sound of birds is heard. Everything freezes. VICTORIA looks at her surroundings.)

VICTORIA
No...

(CAROLINE appears in silhouette.)

CAROLINE
Victoria.

(A bell tolls.)

VICTORIA
How strangely our souls are constructed. By such slight ligaments are we bound to prosperity... or ruin.

CAROLINE
Victoria.

(A bell tolls. VICTORIA turns to look at CAROLINE.)

CAROLINE
Oh, Lord, give me the strength to speak the words. William! That dear, sweet child who kept my heart alive these long and bitter months... Victoria, he is dead!

(All goes dark except for a single light on VICTORIA.)

VICTORIA
We see what we want to see. Tell ourselves the stories we

wish to hear. Yet still… Destiny marches on.

(The world lurches and suddenly VICTORIA is at home. CAROLINE holds the limp body of WILLIAM in her arms. HELENA and ERICH comfort her. VICTORIA stands apart.)

HELENA
(To ERICH) Tell us.

ERICH
We went… We went for a walk. In the woods near Hornbeam.

VICTORIA
Violet House…

CAROLINE
(She speaks almost to herself.) The evening was warm…

ERICH
We walked farther than usual. It was dusk before we thought of returning. Then we discovered that William and Justine—

CAROLINE
They had gone on before. He was playing rabbit again…

ERICH
They were nowhere to be found. We gathered friends. We went out with torches. All night…

CAROLINE
You'll never catch me…

ERICH
Then at five in the morning they found him, stretched on the grass. He had been savagely beaten.

CAROLINE
Oh, God! I have murdered my child! *(The portrait brooch tumbles from her fingers.)*

VICTORIA
What? No!

ERICH
He was wearing the portrait of your father. The frame is gold, solid gold. It was gone, and we think it was this temptation which urged... the murderer to the deed.

VICTORIA
Who? Who was it?

ERICH
Who would believe... Justine could be capable of such a crime?

VICTORIA
Justine? Oh, no!

ERICH
She was found unconscious soon after William was discovered. When she was confined to bed, they found the portrait in her pocket, stained with blood. They questioned her, and her responses were so confused, so strange, that—

CAROLINE
Thank God your father did not live to witness this!

(Lightning flashes and thunder roars. WILLIAM's corpse is carried in procession through the space and lowered into the open grave. CAROLINE, ERICH, and HELENA gather for William's funeral. VICTORIA stands apart.)

ERICH
He was adored by all who knew him.

HELENA
He was so gentle.

CAROLINE
He was the meekest bud, and we failed to shelter him.

(She breaks down in tears. HELENA and ERICH comfort her as they exit. VICTORIA contemplates the grave for a moment.)

VICTORIA
And so my innocence is lost and the scales fall from my eyes. I am not the hero of this story, the story of my life. I am something else. I am…

(The CREATURE appears. It is even larger now. It approaches the grave and gestures. WILLIAM rises from the grave and joins ALPHONSE as puppeteer and voice for the CREATURE. The CREATURE tests its new mobility. Then it speaks, using the voices of ALPHONSE and WILLIAM in perfect unison.)

CREATURE (ALPHONSE/WILLIAM)
Will you now give me what I need?

VICTORIA
I… I can't.

(VICTORIA turns away. The world shifts. ERICH appears and embraces VICTORIA. The CREATURE is gone.)

ERICH
Ah, Victoria; I wish you'd come home months ago.

VICTORIA
It was more than I could bear.

ERICH
I know. But your mother… She grows worse every day.

VICTORIA
I'm... *(Beat)* I'm so sorry.

(The CREATURE's candlelight heart lurks at the edge of the stage. VICTORIA starts.)

ERICH
Victoria?

(VICTORIA looks back and the light is gone.)

VICTORIA
Is this real?

ERICH
What do you mean?

VICTORIA
Is this happening?

ERICH
Victoria, where are you?

VICTORIA
(Shaking off her confusion) Justine is innocent.

ERICH
I know you want to believe that—

VICTORIA
I know it. Have you seen... *(She is uncertain of how to broach the subject.)* Any one unusual?

ERICH
Victoria. Shhh...

VICTORIA
I'm not crazy. Listen to me. Justine is innocent. We have to do something.

ERICH
There's nothing to be done.

VICTORIA
There must be something. *(An idea dawns)* I will confess to the crime.

ERICH
What?! No!

VICTORIA
I would rather confess a thousand times than watch an innocent—

ERICH
You weren't even here when it happened. No one would believe you.

VICTORIA
It wasn't her! I... I know the murderer.

ERICH
No. Victoria, listen to yourself—

VICTORIA
She's innocent!

ERICH
If she is, then I hope, I sincerely hope, she will be acquitted.

VICTORIA
But what do we do?

ERICH
There's nothing to be done.

VICTORIA
Nothing? I cannot do nothing.

ERICH
Then pray. Pray with me.

(JUSTINE appears, holding her cross.)

ERICH
It's what she'd want us to do. Come.

(JUSTINE crosses to sit in a chair perched high atop the pile of rubble. As she walks, VICTORIA and ERICH take a knee. VICTORIA, ERICH, and JUSTINE are isolated in shafts of light. As the prayer begins, ERICH and JUSTINE close their eyes. VICTORIA's eyes remain open and she fights against the moment. Eventually, she commits to the prayer and lights and music change to reflect this.)

JUSTINE
Heavenly Father.

ERICH
We are lost and know not the way.

VICTORIA
(To herself) I can't speak publicly. What would I say? I made a monster? My words would be looked upon as madness.

JUSTINE
Forgive us our doubts.

ERICH
And open our hearts to the righteous certainty of Your love.

VICTORIA
(To herself) But I know she is guiltless. I know the... creature... killed William. And I know it somehow framed Justine. I know it!

JUSTINE
May Your light pierce the shadows that shroud us.

VICTORIA
(To herself) If she is innocent, then... *(A discovery)* Then

I needn't fear any evidence can be brought to actually convict her.

ERICH
May Your love lead us to the truth.

VICTORIA
(To herself) The truth is, they can't convict her. It's impossible.

JUSTINE
Hear our prayer.

VICTORIA
(A realization) I must believe.

ERICH & JUSTINE
Hear our prayer.

VICTORIA
I will believe.

VICTORIA, ERICH & JUSTINE
Hear our prayer.

JUSTINE
Almighty Father, lift us from the darkness.

VICTORIA
We have not only lost that sweet, innocent child, but now Justine is threatened by an even worse fate. If she is condemned, my faith will die. But I am...

JUSTINE
I am certain of Your mercy. For in You, all things are possible.

ERICH & VICTORIA
Amen.

(The prayer ends. VICTORIA and ERICH kneel in

silence for a moment.)

VICTORIA
All will be well.

ERICH
Let's go to the trial.

(A wrenching shift accompanies the noise of crowds and a banging gavel, and they are at the trial: an unnatural proceeding draped in shadow and confusion. The only people clearly seen are JUSTINE, radiating innocence high up in the dock; VICTORIA, standing in misery next to ERICH in the stands; and the CREATURE, looming in the judge's box.)

CREATURE (ALPHONSE/WILLIAM)
How does the accused answer the charges made against her?

JUSTINE
God knows I am innocent. I hope the character I have always borne will incline the court to a favorable—

CREATURE (ALPHONSE/WILLIAM)
Answer the charges!

VICTORIA
Let her speak, for God's sake!

JUSTINE
I lost sight of him. He runs so fast when he plays rabbit. Played rabbit. I searched for him. Searched till I was faint with hunger. But it wasn't enough. It wasn't enough. I pushed myself so hard I collapsed. I know how it looks, my possession of the picture... and the blood... but I can't explain it. Did the murderer place it in my pocket? How? And why? Enough. I commit my soul to the justice of the court.

(Beat)

CREATURE (ALPHONSE/WILLIAM)
Guilty.

(Noise and confusion. VICTORIA reels.)

VICTORIA
No!

CREATURE (ALPHONSE/WILLIAM)
You will be taken from this place to the place whence you came. You will be kept there in close confinement for six days and six nights.

VICTORIA
No! Let me speak!

CREATURE (ALPHONSE/WILLIAM)
On the seventh day, you will be taken to the place of execution.

VICTORIA
I have a confession!

CREATURE (ALPHONSE/WILLIAM)
There you will be hanged by the neck until dead.

VICTORIA
Stop this!

CREATURE (ALPHONSE/WILLIAM)
May God have mercy on your soul.

(A scaffold is erected amidst the rubble and JUSTINE climbs upon it. A rope is strung about her neck. VICTORIA watches from a distance.)

VICTORIA
Justine! Forgive me!

JUSTINE
I'm not afraid to die. God raises my weakness and gives me courage to endure the worst. Learn from me,Victoria, to submit in patience to the will of Heaven.

VICTORIA
Submit?! To a gross injustice?

JUSTINE
May this be the last sorrow you ever suffer.Trust. Believe. Hope.

(JUSTINE is hung by the rope. She twitches, kicks, and then dies. Her body is lowered into the grave. VICTORIA is left alone beside the grave.)

VICTORIA
My faith is lost and I see clearly now. God won't fix this. I must fix this.

(The CREATURE approaches and gestures. JUSTINE rises from the grave and joins it.)

CREATURE (ALPHONSE/WILLIAM/JUSTINE)
Have we now suffered enough?

VICTORIA
(To herself) I must fix this...

CREATURE (ALPHONSE/WILLIAM/JUSTINE)
I am your responsibility.

VICTORIA
(To herself) I must fix this...

CREATURE (ALPHONSE/WILLIAM/JUSTINE)
I am malicious only because I am alone!

VICTORIA
Then what if I... *(A sudden inspiration strikes)* Make another. A creature like yourself. A companion with

whom you can exchange those sympathies necessary for existence...

CREATURE (ALPHONSE/WILLIAM/JUSTINE)
A companion...

VICTORIA
Yes! And I can do better this time. It could be beautiful. It could be an angel.

CREATURE (ALPHONSE/WILLIAM/JUSTINE)
You don't have it in you.

VICTORIA
I do!

CREATURE (ALPHONSE/WILLIAM/JUSTINE)
It will fix nothing.

VICTORIA
It will fix everything! But if I do this, you must go into the wilds and disappear.

CREATURE (ALPHONSE/WILLIAM/JUSTINE)
We would be monsters, cut off from the world.

VICTORIA
But you would be together. You would have...

CREATURE (ALPHONSE/WILLIAM/JUSTINE)
Communion.

(The CREATURE is torn.)

VICTORIA
Swear. Swear that with the companion I bestow you will disappear. Your existence will pass secretly and quietly away. I will never see you or hear you again. It will be as if you never existed. Swear to me.

CREATURE (ALPHONSE/WILLIAM/JUSTINE)
I swear. By the fires of love that burn in my heart. Go; commence your labors. I shall watch your progress. When you are ready I will appear.

(The CREATURE exits. ERICH returns.)

ERICH
Victoria? Come, you should leave this place.

VICTORIA
How do I survive this? Tell me how I'm supposed to survive this.

ERICH
I won't tell you that we're given only what we can manage. We both know that's a lie. But I will tell you what I believe. While we love, while we are true to one other, I believe that together we can survive anything.

VICTORIA
Promise me.

ERICH
What shall I promise you?

VICTORIA
That you will be my husband. If I can't trust in God or justice, then I must have a companion, a hope for the future.

(ERICH considers before responding.)

ERICH
I have known love. Profound love. I have cried in your mother's arms. I've laughed with your father beside the fire. I've held Justine's hand on a midnight walk and cleaned William's knees after a tumble in the woods. And in your absence I have taken lovers. But they were

not for me. And I was not for them. What we share... It is a feeling with no equal on this earth. Which is a terrible burden, for I know you don't feel as I do.

VICTORIA
No, I—

ERICH
Don't. Our marriage was your parents' favorite dream. They told us this since we were children, taught us to view it as inevitable. But you've spent so much time away.

VICTORIA
Erich...

ERICH
I confess to you, my friend, my best friend, that I love you. But our marriage would destroy me if it were not the result of your own free choice. So, Victoria, I ask you: what is it you wish?

(Beat)

VICTORIA
I want to be your wife. For as long as we both shall live.

(Beat)

ERICH
Then I will be your husband.

VICTORIA
There is something I must do first. It will take... some time.

ERICH
How long?

VICTORIA
I don't know. But then it will be over and we will be

together. Forever.

(VICTORIA kisses ERICH. Lights shift. ERICH has disappeared.)

VICTORIA
I have a duty to perform. The sooner I make this companion, the sooner it will all be over. I go to work.

(VICTORIA travels to school with HELENA. She collects objects from the rubble and piles them together, trying to avoid HELENA's attention.)

VICTORIA
It is like the torture of single drops falling continually on my head. Drop. Drop. Drop. Every thought is a misery. My heart cannot withstand the pressure. Yet I work.

(VICTORIA contemplates the collected pieces. There is nothing of significance; it's merely rubbish. HELENA enters the space and VICTORIA is forced to conceal her work.)

VICTORIA
Helena feels the need to observe me now, at all hours of the day, and this arrangement proves impractical. I must have solitude. I must have secrecy.

(VICTORIA crosses to her little cottage.)

VICTORIA
I return to my cabin in the mountains, the remotest spot I can imagine. I tell Helena I wish to view the wonders of Nature for a time. I tell her it will bring me peace. She assists me with my move.

(HELENA joins VICTORIA. They step out of the cottage and HELENA is dazzled by the view.)

HELENA
You know, Victoria, I have seen the most beautiful sights of our country. I have swum in the lakes and the harbors; I have walked through the deep woods, waded the streams, and gamboled through the great fields that blanket the valleys. But this place pleases me more than all those wonders. These mountains are so majestic. There is a charm to the trees and the foliage. The sounding cataract haunts me like a passion; the tall rocks, their colors and their forms, are to me an appetite, a feeling, that has no equal anywhere else on this earth. Ah! Pardon my outpouring of emotion.

VICTORIA
(Embracing HELENA) No. Don't apologize. Our separation will not last long. I need you, Helena. I don't say it often enough. I need you.

HELENA
Victoria?

VICTORIA
Yes?

HELENA
Live. Choose to live.

(HELENA exits.)

VICTORIA
I have a duty to perform.

(VICTORIA assembles her collected objects into humanoid shape. She rifles through her journal, looking for inspiration. The CREATURE enters and watches through its chink in the wall.)

VICTORIA
Sometimes I cannot bear to work at all. At other times I

toil day and night in order to complete my task: It's not working. There's nothing left inside me. The heavens are dark. And a question haunts me. *(She is still for a time.)* I once created a fiend. *(Taking a burning log from the fireplace)* Will I now truly form another?

(She lights her new creation on fire. As flames dance with hellish fury, the CREATURE enters.)

VICTORIA
(Lighting more and more of it on fire.) Never again. Never again. *(Tossing her journal into the flames)* Never again!

CREATURE (ALPHONSE/WILLIAM/JUSTINE)
I told you. I told you! You don't have it in you. Now embrace me!

VICTORIA
There must be another way.

CREATURE (ALPHONSE/WILLIAM/JUSTINE)
There is no other way!

VICTORIA
I will find it.

CREATURE (ALPHONSE/WILLIAM/JUSTINE)
You turn to your friends. You turn to your family. You turn to this... You turn to everyone but me! Why do you hate me?

VICTORIA
I don't... hate you. I don't even—

CREATURE (ALPHONSE/WILLIAM/JUSTINE)
You do! What will it take? What must I burn to make you love me? See me!

VICTORIA
No...

CREATURE (ALPHONSE/WILLIAM/JUSTINE)
Hear me!

VICTORIA
No...

CREATURE (ALPHONSE/WILLIAM/JUSTINE)
Help me!

VICTORIA
No!

(Beat)

CREATURE (ALPHONSE/WILLIAM/JUSTINE)
Then so be it.

(The CREATURE exits. VICTORIA races back to school.)

VICTORIA
I need help. I have to get to Helena. We'll go home. We'll tell Erich. We'll make a plan. We'll figure this out. Together we can survive anything. I reach our apartments.

(VICTORIA arrives at her apartment. All is dark and still.)

VICTORIA
Helena?

(VICTORIA moves cautiously forward. After a beat, she hears a faint, muffled cry.)

VICTORIA
Helena! Where are you?

(VICTORIA crosses to a window and throws open the curtains. Dim evening light spills into the room.

VICTORIA sees HELENA being held tight by the CREATURE, its hand over her mouth. HELENA cries out and struggles, but the CREATURE violently tightens its grip.)

VICTORIA
No! Not Helena!

CREATURE (ALPHONSE/WILLIAM/JUSTINE)
Shall you know friendship and love, and I be alone?

VICTORIA
How did you get in here?

CREATURE (ALPHONSE/WILLIAM/JUSTINE)
It's too easy. They're all so ignorant of what you are. And what you've done. They don't know to fear. To fear you. To fear me. And so I come.

VICTORIA
You don't have to do this!

CREATURE (ALPHONSE/WILLIAM/JUSTINE)
And so they fall.

VICTORIA
I'm begging you—

CREATURE (ALPHONSE/WILLIAM/JUSTINE)
And you could have stopped this.

(The CREATURE points at VICTORIA at the end of its line, uncovering HELENA's mouth.)

VICTORIA
Please, no, no, no—

HELENA
Victoria! Nothing inside you can truly die unless—

(The CREATURE suddenly and violently snaps

HELENA's neck and drops her into the grave.)

VICTORIA
I will never feel joy again. I see this clearly now.

CREATURE (ALPHONSE/WILLIAM/JUSTINE)
Now you feel what I feel.

(HELENA rises from the grave and joins the CREATURE.)

CREATURE (ALPHONSE/WILLIAM/JUSTINE/HELENA)
I will never stop. I will take and take. I will destroy your past. I will consume your future.

VICTORIA
What!? No! The future is safe. It's supposed to be safe!

CREATURE (ALPHONSE/WILLIAM/JUSTINE/HELENA)
And I will be with you on your wedding night.

(The CREATURE exits.)

VICTORIA
My duty is clear: save Erich. Save Erich. Save Erich. I know when it's coming now. I can prepare. I can make ready.

(The world lurches. VICTORIA is at home, with ERICH.)

ERICH
(Embracing her) Oh, my love, how have you suffered!

VICTORIA
Everything that's happened is my fault.

ERICH
Tell me what's wrong.

(VICTORIA sees the CREATURE's candlelight heart looming at the edge of the stage.)

ERICH
Victoria. Tell me.

(VICTORIA sees the CREATURE's heart in another location.)

VICTORIA
I have a secret, Erich, a dreadful one.

(VICTORIA sees the CREATURE's heart everywhere she looks.)

ERICH
What is it?

VICTORIA
I promise I'll confide it to you on the night of our wedding. But until then, please, don't ask me to speak of it.

ERICH
I can help.

VICTORIA
No one can help me. Not with this.

ERICH
You have to let me in.

VICTORIA
No. This is me. This is mine. It's not something you can fix. Respect me in this.

(Beat)

ERICH
Victoria?

VICTORIA
Yes?

ERICH
Live. Choose to live.

(Time passes as ERICH and CAROLINE put up wedding decorations, all in blacks and grays.)

VICTORIA
I agree to my mother's elaborate wedding plans, though they may only serve as decoration to a tragedy. The church is arranged, the wine procured. Preparations are made. Congratulatory visits are received. Everyone smiles. I shut up in my heart the anxiety that preys there and show them the face they want to see.

(Lights shift. VICTORIA stands in an empty void.)

VICTORIA
Meanwhile, I prepare myself for what I must do.

(She produces a pistol and contemplates it in silence for a moment.)

VICTORIA
People die. Every day. Geniuses. Visionaries. The kindest and noblest of heart. Yet I live. I. Live. Where is the justice in that? *(She puts the pistol away.)* But this one task remains before me: I will destroy the monster I created. This one worthwhile thing will I do.

(A wedding ceremony is set beneath gloomy skies and distant thunder. Faceless guests lurk in the darkness. ERICH stands before a PRIEST. CAROLINE is close by. VICTORIA joins ERICH.)

PRIEST
Before Almighty God, state your intentions. Have you

come to enter into this marriage without coercion, freely and wholeheartedly?

VICTORIA & ERICH
I have.

PRIEST
Are you prepared to love and honor one another?

VICTORIA & ERICH
For as long as we both shall live.

PRIEST
Join hands.

VICTORIA & ERICH
I will be faithful, in sickness and in health, till death do us part.

PRIEST
What God has joined, let no one put asunder.

(Thunder and lightning. The world lurches. VICTORIA and ERICH stand by the lake. Watery light radiates upward from the open grave.)

VICTORIA
We travel to Violet House. It is my mother's wedding gift to us. She spends her remaining fortune on it, that we might start our new life in the home of our dreams, rather than the cradle of our sorrows. Standing by the water's edge, my husband's hand in mine, I almost feel... something. But first...

(VICTORIA crosses away and draws her pistol, keeping it hidden from ERICH.)

VICTORIA
Come, my love. There is something we must face.

ERICH
Victoria?

VICTORIA
It's waiting up at the house. Waiting for both of us. But together we can survive anything. This will all be over soon.

(VICTORIA walks towards the house. ERICH starts to follow when, with a terrible crash of thunder and lightning, the CREATURE rears out of the grave and envelops ERICH.)

ERICH
Victoria!

(ERICH is pulled under the water and out of sight. The CREATURE's heart appears across the stage. VICTORIA fires the pistol at it. The heart appears in another location. VICTORIA fires. Again and again, the heart appears, but VICTORIA can't hit it. She collapses.)

(The real CREATURE enters. ERICH rises from the grave and joins it.)

(CAROLINE enters. She approaches VICTORIA but VICTORIA turns away. CAROLINE begins pulling down the wedding decorations as the CREATURE watches.)

CAROLINE
I dreamt last night of your father.

VICTORIA
All hope is gone...

CAROLINE
It was before you were born. Before we opened our hearts and our home to so many precious little souls.

Before we set aside who we were and what we wanted for who you needed us to be.

VICTORIA
All light is gone...

CAROLINE
I would never have chosen another life. Never. I would never have chosen to give up the joys we shared as a family. Or so I always thought. But now, I wonder.

(CAROLINE pulls out a small vial of dark liquid.)

VICTORIA
I can see no further than the outer limits of my own pain...

CAROLINE
I wonder what I wouldn't give up for one more moment as it was. With him. Before. To return to our wedding night and start again. To build a new life. *(She drinks from the vial.)* For ourselves.

(Music plays. The CREATURE approaches CAROLINE and bows, extending a hand.)

VICTORIA
And then my mother departs. And her soul joins with his.

(CAROLINE dances with the CREATURE. It is beautiful. At the end of the dance, CAROLINE joins the operation of the CREATURE.)

CREATURE (ALPHONSE/WILL/JUST/HELENA/ERICH/CAROLINE)
Will you now give me what I need?

VICTORIA
And something finally breaks through. My pain is not all there is.

CREATURE (ALPHONSE/WILL/JUST/HELENA/ERICH/CAROLINE)
Give me what I need.

VICTORIA
There is more. There is more. There always has been. And it's out there.

CREATURE (ALPHONSE/WILL/JUST/HELENA/ERICH/CAROLINE)
Give me what I need.

VICTORIA
I just can't see it from the rubble of my wasted life. So I take a step. And then another. And then... *(A release)* I leave it all behind.

(VICTORIA travels into uncharted territory. Journal pages begin to fall from the sky, tumbling like snow, blanketing the stage. The CREATURE follows VICTORIA, but falls behind.)

VICTORIA
I run. Farther and farther. Higher and higher. And it all falls away. Farther and farther. Higher and higher.

(She stops. All is still. All is silent. VICTORIA sinks to the ground.)

VICTORIA
And then, when I've run as far and as high as I can go, I see everything laid out before me. And there it is.

(The quality of light begins to change into something brighter and cleaner than ever before. VICTORIA takes in the sight of her CREATURE from a distance and standing there among her family, it seems less menacing and more human.)

VICTORIA
My creature. My creation. My... miracle. For it is a miracle. Flawed. And sad. And broken. And mine. I stop fight-

ing. And, at last... I surrender. I surrender. I surrender.

(The CREATURE extends a hand and VICTORIA approaches. The CREATURE folds VICTORIA into its powerful arms. For the first time, VICTORIA weeps. She weeps with abandon, cradled in the CREATURE's care.)

CREATURE (ALPHONSE/WILL/JUST/HELENA/ERICH/CAROLINE)
I know. I know. Nothing is so painful as a great and sudden change.

VICTORIA
He is gone. Forever.

CREATURE (ALPHONSE/WILL/JUST/HELENA/ERICH/CAROLINE)
Life is a treasure of great value. Its loss is a wound most touching. *(Beat.)* But wounds can heal.

(A transformation occurs within VICTORIA.)

VICTORIA
Wounds can heal...

CREATURE (ALPHONSE/WILL/JUST/HELENA/ERICH/CAROLINE)
Yes.

(CAROLINE, ERICH, HELENA, JUSTINE, and WILLIAM lay a hand on ALPHONSE. After this, the CREATURE only speaks with ALPHONSE's voice.)

CREATURE (ALPHONSE)
Are you ready now?

VICTORIA
I... am.

CREATURE (ALPHONSE)
Then tell me: what am I?

VICTORIA
You are... what I made you.

CREATURE (ALPHONSE)
Yes. And you understand that I'll never stop.

VICTORIA
I know.

CREATURE (ALPHONSE)
I will ask more than you can give.

VICTORIA
I know. *(A further awakening)* But it's not your fault.

CREATURE (Alphonse)
No.

VICTORIA
It is, however, my responsibility.

CREATURE (ALPHONSE)
Yes.

(VICTORIA stands and brings the CREATURE to its feet. She stands before it and looks directly into its face, perhaps for the first time.)

VICTORIA
I see you. I hear you. I own you.

(She embraces the CREATURE.)

VICTORIA
And now...

VICTORIA & CREATURE (ALPHONSE)
It's time.

(Piece by piece, VICTORIA disassembles the CREATURE. As she removes the piece operated by

CAROLINE, CAROLINE steps away and sets it aside. The same happens with ERICH, HELENA, JUSTINE, and WILLIAM and they come to form a ring around VICTORIA and ALPHONSE. ALPHONSE takes the candle from heart of the puppet and hands it to VICTORIA.)

VICTORIA
My father is dead.

ALPHONSE
But you will survive. You are not alone.

(VICTORIA blows out the candle. A vast sea of stars ignites in the heavens. The family stands in their light.)

VICTORIA
There is hope.

END OF PLAY

ABOUT THE PLAYWRIGHT

Robert Kauzlaric is a Chicago-based playwright, actor, and director.

He is a proud Ensemble Member of Lifeline Theatre and Irish Theatre of Chicago, and Artistic Associate of the Michigan Shakespeare Festival.

Robert has written more than a dozen theatrical adaptations which have been performed in over forty states across the U.S., as well as in Australia, Canada, England, and Ireland.

The *New York Times* called his adaptation of ***The True Story of the 3 Little Pigs!*** "One of the best children's shows of the year." His version of H.G. Wells' ***The Island of Dr. Moreau*** received five of Chicago's Non-Equity Jeff Awards, including New Adaptation and Best Production; his adaptation of Neil Gaiman's ***Neverwhere*** received the Non-Equity Jeff Award for New Adaptation; and his version of Jane Austen's ***Northanger Abbey*** (with composer George Howe) received the Non-Equity Jeff Award for New Work–Musical. He was commissioned by the Illinois Shakespeare Festival to produce a new adaptation of Dumas' ***The Three Musketeers***. Four of his plays are licensed by Playscripts, Inc, three have been published by Sordelet Ink, and he has been published in Dramatics Magazine.

PLAYSCRIPTS FROM SORDELET INK

Action Movie—The Play by Joe Foust and Richard Ragsdale
All Childish Things by Joseph Zettelmaier
Captain Blood adapted by David Rice
the Count of Monte Cristo adapted by Christopher M Walsh
Dead Man's Shoes by Joseph Zettelmaier
The Decade Dance by Joseph Zettelmaier
Ebenezer: a christmas play by Joseph Zettelmaier
Eve of Ides—a play by David Blixt
Frankenstein adapted by Robert Kauzlaric
The Gravedigger: a frankenstein play by Joseph Zettelmaier
Hatfield & McCoy by Shawn Pfautsch
Haunted by Joseph Zettelmaier
Her Majesty's Will adapted by Robert Kauzlaric
It Came From Mars by Joseph Zettelmaier
the League of Awesome by Corrbette Pasko and Sara Sevigny
the Moonstone adapted by Robert Kauzlaric
Northern Aggression by Joseph Zettelmaier
Once A Ponzi Time by Joe Foust
The Renaissance Man by Joseph Zettelmaier
The Scullery Maid by Joseph Zettelmaier
Anton Chekhov's the Seagull adapted by Janice L Blixt
Season on the Line by Shawn Pfautsch
Stage Fright: a horror anthology by Joseph Zettelmaier
a Tale of Two Cities adapted by Christopher M Walsh
Voices in the Dark by Joseph Zettelmaier
Williamston Anthology: Volume 1
Williamston Anthology: Volume 2

Sordelet Ink Novels by David Blixt

Nellie Bly

What Girls Are Good For

Charity Girl

Clever Girl

The Star-Cross'd Series

The Master Of Verona

Voice Of The Falconer

Fortune's Fool

The Prince's Doom

Varnish'd Faces: Star-Cross'd Short Stories

Will & Kit

Her Majesty's Will

The Colossus Series

Colossus: Stone & Steel

Colossus: The Four Emperors

Eve of Ides—a play

non-fiction

Shakespeare's Secrets: Romeo & Juliet

Tomorrow, and Tomorrow: Essays on Macbeth

Fighting Words

THE MYSTERY OF CENTRAL PARK

A rejected marriage proposal and the corpse of a dead beauty confound Dick Treadwell's hopes for happiness, until his beloved Penelope sets him a task: she will marry him if he solves—*the Mystery of Central Park!*

EVA, THE ADVENTURESS

Nellie Bly's ripped-from-the-headlines novel of a poor girl determined to revenge herself upon the world, only to find that, in the battle between love and revenge, only one can triumph.

NEW YORK BY NIGHT

Setting out to solve the bold diamond robbery, millionaire detective Lionel Dangerfield finds himself in competition with Ruby Sharpe, daring young reporter for the *New York Planet.* Will "The Danger" solve the case before Ruby can steal the story—and his heart?

ALTA LYNN, M.D.

A prank goes awry and Alta Lynn finds herself wed against her will. Leaving love behind, she throws herself into the study of medicine, only to find that love has other plans for her!

WAYNE'S FAITHFUL SWEETHEART

Beautiful Dorette Lover is rescued from poverty when she finds work as an artist's model. That same day she witnesses a seeming murder. To protect the man accused, she agrees to become his bride—only to fall desperately in love with him!

LITTLE LUCKIE

Luckie Thurlow longs to be accepted by society and gain the man she loves. But she harbors a dark secret—she is the daughter of the murderous Gypsy Queen, who plans to use Luckie to gain her own revenge!

IN LOVE WITH A STRANGER

Kit Clarendon is in love! Trouble is, she doesn't know her love's name. But she is determined to track him down and force him to love her! A wild pursuit filled with disguises, desperate deeds, and declarations of love as Kit determines to go through fire and water to win him!

THE LOVE OF THREE GIRLS

An heiress in disguise, a factory girl with dreams of wealth, and a sweet child of charity are forced into rivalry when they all fall in love with the same man! Murder, fever, fallen women, and a desperate villain conspire against—*the love of three girls!*

www.ingramcontent.com/pod-product-compliance
Lightning Source LLC
LaVergne TN
LVHW050939080826
845145LV00004B/1330

* 9 7 8 1 9 4 4 5 4 0 9 6 8 *